Tiddlers

Feet!

by Barrie Wade

Illustrated by Rocket Cartoons

W

Notes on the series

TIDDLERS are structured to provide support for children who are starting to read on their own. The stories may also be used for sharing with children.

Starting to read alone can be daunting. **TIDDLERS** help by listing the words in the book for a check before reading, and by providing visual support and repeating words and phrases. These books will both develop confidence and encourage reading and rereading for pleasure.

If you are reading this book with a child, here are a few suggestions:

1. Make reading fun! Choose a time to read when you and the child are relaxed and have time to share the story.
2. Talk about the story before you start reading. Look at the cover and the blurb. What might the story be about? Why might the child like it?
3. Look also at the list of words below – can the child tackle most of the words? Encourage the child to employ a phonics approach to tackling new words by sounding the words out.
4. Encourage the child to retell the story, using the jumbled picture puzzle.
5. Give praise! Remember that small mistakes need not always be corrected.

Here is a list of the words in this story.

Common words:

and	don't	lots
all	have	of
at	I	no
big	little	

Other words:

care	feet	slow
cold	four	two
fast	hot	

I have little feet.

I have big feet.

I have fast feet.

I have slow feet.

I have hot feet.

I have cold feet.

13

I have two feet.

I have four feet.

I have lots of feet.

I have no feet at all
and I don't care!

a

b

Can you find these
pictures in the story?

Which pages are the pictures from?

Turn over for answers!

Answers

The pictures come from these pages:

a. pages 12–13

b. pages 6–7

c. pages 14–15

d. pages 8–9

Franklin Watts
First published in Great Britain in 2016 by
The Watts Publishing Group

Copyright (text) © Barrie Wade 2016
Copyright (illustration) © Rocket Cartoons 2016

The rights of Barrie Wade to be identified as the author and Rocket Cartoons to be identified as the illustrators of this Work have been asserted in accordance with the Copyright, Designs and Patents Act, 1988.

Series Editor: Jackie Hamley
Series Advisor: Catherine Glavina
Series Designer: Cathryn Gilbert

A CIP catalogue record for this book is available from the British Library.

ISBN 978 1 4451 4500 6 (hbk)
ISBN 978 1 4451 4503 7 (pbk)
ISBN 978 1 4451 4501 3 (library ebook)

Printed in China

Franklin Watts
An imprint of
Hachette Children's Group
Part of The Watts Publishing Group
Carmelite House
50 Victoria Embankment
London EC4Y 0DZ

An Hachette UK Company
www.hachette.co.uk

www.franklinwatts.co.uk